Two Much for You

SKY CORGAN

Copyright © 2017 Sky Corgan

All rights reserved.

ISBN: 9781520486864

CONTENTS

Chapter One	1
Chapter Two	7
Chapter Three	15
Chapter Four	23
Chapter Five	28
Chapter Six	34
Chapter Seven	38

CHAPTER ONE
ROSE

Is it wrong to spy on your next door neighbor with binoculars? And by spy, I mean peek through the blinds of your second story window with your tongue lolling out while you watch loads of shirtless hot muscle suds-downed and scrubbing a Camaro in the summer heat. Soap tastes like shit, but I'd love to lick the glistening wetness off of every inch of my new neighbors' torso.

Both of them.

What bros. I smirk to myself as neighbor number two comes out of the house like he's getting ready to step onto the photo shoot of a fireman calendar. Ripped faded jeans. Perfectly styled blonde hair. And what do you know. No shirt.

My face hurts from all the grinning as I eye him lecherously, thinking about what I could do to that body.

They're a perfect pair. One brunette, one blond. One broad and chiseled, the other lean and cut. Both of them could be models. Hell, they might be for all I know. They both drive nice cars. Both have looks that kill. Both have filled my fantasies at night ever since they moved in two weeks ago.

I wet my lips with my tongue as I watch Mr. Blond grab a sponge from the soap bucket to help his buddy out. They have to be gay, I realize with a slight frown. They're too beautiful, and I've never seen two guys wash a car together like this before.

I pull my fingers out from between the blinds and listen to the metallic sound of them snapping shut, then I turn and press my back against the wall, inhaling deeply. Just watching the two of them has me turned on. Too bad it's all for naught. Even if they weren't gay, it would be all for naught. Realistically, I wouldn't have a chance with either one of them. They're too perfect, and I highly doubt I'm the type of girl they'd go for.

My eyes drift down to my less than flat stomach. I'm far from fat, but I could certainly afford to lose a few pounds. Guys like them probably date stick skinny girls with perfect hair, flawless makeup, and giant breasts. At least, I have one of those three things going for me.

I cup my tits and readjust them in the old sports bra I'm wearing. The poor thing has seen so many miles that the elastic in it is just about shot. I need to get rid of it, but it's one of my most comfortable bras, and I don't see the harm in walking around the house in it. Besides, it's not like anyone else will ever see it. Not like *they* will ever see it.

I chew my bottom lip for a moment before giving in to the urge to peek at my neighbors again. One is stretching out over the hood while the other is scrubbing down the trunk. I sigh as I watch their bodies glisten from the tiny water droplets beading their skin.

Maybe I should put some clothes on and go over to introduce myself. That is the neighborly thing to do, after all. I had told myself that's exactly what I would do when I found out that new people were moving in next door...until I saw how gorgeous they were.

To be fair, I did give it a try. A few days after they moved in I baked them chocolate chip cookies. I got dressed in my workout clothes and pulled my long brown hair up into a high ponytail, hoping to impress them by making them think I care about fitness. It's not really a lie. Does going to the gym once a week with my best friend qualify as caring about fitness?

I had given myself a pep talk as I walked with the cookies to the front door. But as soon as I opened the door and my eyes landed on my dark-haired neighbor working on his car in his driveway, my cheeks turned about fifty shades of pink and I immediately did a u-turn back into my house. Then my mind went wild with excuses for why I shouldn't go over. Things like, *he looks busy. Maybe I should try another time.* And, *both of them have less than ten percent body fat. They probably don't even eat cookies.*

The cookies sat in my kitchen for days before frustration and temptation got the best of me and I ended up eating the whole plate by myself while sitting on my sofa brooding over my shyness. I knew then what the real excuse was. The odds of me trying to talk to them without blushing like my face was on fire were slim to none. It's always been an uncontrollable reaction I've had to stunningly attractive men—a dead giveaway of my thoughts about them. That is a super awkward way to start a relationship with your neighbors. It's better if they just remain strangers, to save myself some embarrassment.

I sigh, letting my desire to get to know them fade away. I can stare and try to motivate myself all day, but that's not going to make my feet carry me over to their house. Maybe someday we'll cross paths, but it's not going to be today.

My blond neighbor glances over his shoulder up towards my window and my breath hitches as our eyes meet. At least, I think our eyes met. I withdrew from the blinds like they bit me, jumping back a good foot.

It looks like I embarrassed myself anyway. He totally just caught me spying on them.

For a moment, I feel panicked. But then I decide to let it go. Who cares if he saw me staring? They're both half-naked and yummy. What straight woman wouldn't be trying to catch a peek if she had such a good view? Besides, it's not like I was taking pictures or video or anything(though now that I think about it, that would have been a brilliant idea). No harm. No foul.

I stand there until the rhythm of my heart returns to normal, then I concede defeat and head back downstairs to find my cell phone. Seeing the two of them was a painful reminder of what's missing from my life.

Dick.

No. That's just my hormones talking. I want a boyfriend. I've wanted a boyfriend for the past several months.

Jumping back into the dating game after five years of being single was so much harder than I ever thought it would be. It's not so much that finding guys to date is difficult, it's finding quality guys. And by quality guys, I mean guys who aren't just out to fuck and run.

Now that I've hit my thirties, it seems like everyone is coming out of divorces and looking to sow some wild oats. Meanwhile, I'm on the other end of things, ready to find someone to settle down with. Never in a million years did I think I'd still be single at this age. But here I am, spending my nights on the sofa having regular threesomes with Ben and Jerry because all the guys I meet are players or losers.

Just thinking about opening the dating app on my phone makes me want to groan, but then I remind myself that I'm not the sit and wait for it to come to me type of girl. If I'm not proactive about dating, I'll probably be single forever. And surely, I am not the only decent, honest, romance-seeking person on the app. Surely, there's someone else out there looking for love.

I grab my phone and make my way to the sofa in the living room, practically tipping over from sexual frustration when I toss myself down onto it. Damn those guys for getting me all worked up. At least, they motivated me to give this dating thing another try. I've been in give-up mode for the past few days after a less than promising date with a recovering alcoholic who thought he could charm me by telling me how much of an asshole he is. That guy actually wanted to see me again, but I've never been one to chase after bad boys. Life is full of enough drama without knowingly piling someone else's crap on top of my own.

I open up the app and sigh as the first image pops up. My finger is already in swipe to Dislike mode. Dud. Dud. Dud. He's kinda cute. Let's give him a Like and see what happens. Dud. Dud.

Holy shit.

My spine straightens, catapulting me into perfect posture as I gaze down at the screen, my eyes flitting from the picture to the distance from me that this Adonis—these Adonises—live. Less than one mile.

It can't be.

My brain rewinds to a few minutes ago when I was staring out my second story window at my neighbors. I zoom in, trying to capture the details of their faces. There is no doubt in my mind. I'm looking at a picture of them. Both of them. Sitting at a bar, dressed in business suits, smiling at the camera.

I scroll through the rest of the photos trying to figure out which one the profile belongs to. Oddly, every single photo is of both of them. There's no indication that the profile belongs to one or the other.

I glance at the name on the profile and smirk. 2Much4You. Players, the both of them. A screen name like that screams obvious. At least, I know they're not gay now. Or that one of them isn't gay. Though with all of the bro-dum going on in the pictures, one can't help but wonder. Maybe they're brothers. Like, legitimate brothers. One thing is for certain, though, they're definitely attached at the hip.

Curiously, I scroll down to the space designated for their profile description. A soft huff leaves my lips as I find it empty. Typical. So many guys on this app don't even bother. Proof again that they're only looking to get laid.

I squeeze my thighs together, a devious thought corrupting my brain. The image of me sandwiched between them is pleasant. And just looking at them turns me on. Maybe it wouldn't be so bad for me to tap the Like button and see what comes of it.

My finger hovers over the button for a few seconds, my mind going wild with possibilities. Then reality kicks in. If they don't respond or Like me back, not only will my confidence be crushed, but I'll also become paranoid and probably try to avoid them. The thought of being trapped in my house while one or both of them are out in their garage is less than appealing.

The mischievous smirk I was wearing dips into a frown, and I close the app with a sigh. Maybe that one semi-cute guy that I Liked will get back to me. That's the best I can hope for right now.

CHAPTER TWO
GARETH

"Stop dawdling."

I turn just in time to get blasted in the face by the water hose. Devlin is grinning at me, but I'm just annoyed.

"Such gratitude you show me for helping to wash your car." I roll my eyes at him.

"I am being grateful. It's hot. I thought you could use some cooling off." He smirks before tossing the hose down and getting back to work scrubbing the trunk of his car.

"I think we're being spied on." I quickly gesture over my shoulder with my thumb, trying to keep my hand low so that our Peeping Tom doesn't notice.

"By who? Her?" Devlin looks at the house across the street.

"Mhm." I nod before crouching to wipe down the front bumper.

"So?"

"Just thought it was worth mentioning is all." I sigh.

"Every neighborhood has a nosy neighbor. I guess we found ours." He shrugs it off.

"I suppose you're right. It's a pretty quiet

neighborhood. You rarely see anyone outside."

"Well, that's going to change now that we're here."

I snort. "Oh yes, we will be the hated neighbors on the block, always out in the garage on our days off making noise."

"They'll get used to it." Devlin tosses his microfiber sponge into the soap bucket and picks up the hose to rinse the car off. "Are you done?"

"Yup." I stand. "I think I'm going to head in and take a shower."

"Thanks for the help." He doesn't even look at me as he places his finger over the hose opening to make the water come out in a spray.

"No problem." I toss my washcloth into the bucket before heading inside.

Just that short period of time spent in the sun has my body feeling overheated. I turn the shower on to cold and shiver as the water kisses my skin. The stickiness and heat melt away, making me feel instantly better.

Then all of a sudden, the water gets scalding hot.

I cringe and jump out of the shower, cursing Devlin. No doubt, he's in one of the other bathrooms laughing his ass off. Such a dick, that one. I'll get him back though. Maybe stick his hand in warm water while he's sleeping. I could spend an entire year pranking him and still not catch up to all of the hell he's put me through since we met in middle school. Being a practical joker is his thing, though, not mine. I've always been the serious one. Perhaps that's why we balance each other out so well. His weaknesses are my strengths, and my weaknesses are his strengths. He always jokes that together we make the ultimate person. Maybe he's right.

I finish my shower and towel off my short, blond hair before slipping on a pair of boxer briefs and heading into the living room. Devlin is sitting on the sofa grinning up at me like a loon.

"Did you have a nice shower?"

I glare at him. "You wait."

"You always say that." He gestures at me absentmindedly before refocusing his attention on the football game on TV.

I could not care less about football. Especially college football, which is what he's watching. Basketball is my sport. We have a rule, though, that whoever gets to the TV in the living room first gets to pick what we watch. We both have televisions in our bedrooms, so it's not like I couldn't just get up and go to my room. I feel too lazy to move right now, though.

Out of boredom, I grab my phone off of the coffee table and open a game. It's one of those match-three games, a guilty pleasure that I typically only indulge in when I'm waiting around somewhere.

"What are you doing?" Devlin leans over to look at my screen during the commercial break.

"I'm ignoring you. What does it look like I'm doing?" I furrow my brow and tilt the screen away from him.

"Pfft. Playing your little girly games? You should be using your time for more productive things."

"Like?"

"Like finding us a date for tonight." He smirks, putting on his player face. I can't help but laugh at him. He looks so damn cheesy.

"Finding us a date for tonight." I nod. "Does that mean we're looking for hit it and quit it?"

"Naw, man. I thought we talked about this already." His expression twists in offense.

"We did." I exhale deeply as I close the game and pull up the dating app.

To be honest, after nearly six months of unsuccessfully trying to find a girl who wants to be in a relationship with both of us, I've just about given up. It's a lot easier to find someone who just wants to have a threesome. Sex is uncomplicated. But I know deep down that's not what either one of us needs. We need something with more substance. Something regular. Something real.

"I really don't think this is working. Maybe we should try something else." I scan through the girls at a fast pace, not really putting much effort in. Devlin should be the one doing this. He's the one who still has some optimism left.

"Oh, don't look so excited. And don't be so picky." He snatches the phone out of my hand when he realizes I'm not really looking, just going through the motions.

"I'm not being picky. I'm being a realist." I cross my arms over my chest and lean back against the sofa. "Finding a girl who wants to date two men is like looking for a needle in a haystack."

"We found Debra." He doesn't even glance at me, and I cringe knowing that he's Liking every single semi-attractive girl he comes across, trawling the never ending sea of girls in the area, hoping to catch one that's willing to accept the strange arrangement that we want. It's proof that he's starting to wear down too. I can tell, even if he won't admit it.

"Debra." My heart aches as her name rolls off of my tongue. I haven't said it in such a long time—haven't tasted the sweetness of it.

"The one that got away." There's a hint of depression in Devlin's tone.

"Yeah. The one that got away."

I can still remember the day she boarded a plane to go teach English in Japan. We had both loved her, and she had loved us. Because of that love, we let her go. Not like we could have stopped her.

I remember the weeks prior to her leaving spent talking to Devlin about whether or not we should follow her. With my career in the radiology field, I could have easily picked up and left. Devlin is in the army, though, and he couldn't just throw away twelve years of service to chase after her. He tried to get a transfer, but it didn't go through, and he thought it was cruel to make her wait for us for an undetermined amount of time. The selfish part of me thinks we should have asked her to wait—the part of me that was so in love. That seems like a lifetime ago now, even though it's been less than a year.

"I wonder what she's doing right now," I say thoughtfully.

"Probably sandwiched between two Japs, not even thinking about us." He quirks a halfhearted smile.

"That's not even funny." I tilt my head towards him, not appreciating the joke.

The only guys I want to imagine Debra sandwiched between are Devlin and I. For as long as it's been, I can still remember the softness of her skin beneath my fingertips. The taste of her lips. But it feels like those memories are fading with each passing day.

Devlin sets the phone down on his lap for a minute, looking at me seriously. "She's not coming back, Gareth."

"I know." I puff up my cheeks and blow out a painful breath.

"This." He picks back up the phone and shows it to me. "This is our only chance of being happy like that again. We found Debra. We'll find someone else to love us. Even if you are boring as fuck."

His expression cracks in amusement, but I don't smile back. My eyes are fixed on the screen. There's a very familiar face there. One I'm sure I've seen before.

"See, you just proved my point. Laugh once in a while." He frowns, taking the phone back.

"Wait." I pull it away from him before he has a chance to Like the image and move on.

"What?" He furrows his brow at me.

"This girl." I show him the phone. "Doesn't she look familiar to you?"

He leans in and squints for a better look. Then he smiles from ear to ear. "Oh my God. Is that really? Do you think it is?"

"Mhm." I can't help but grin. "It's Mrs. Peeping Tom herself."

"Well, I guess that means she's not married. I rarely see other cars in her driveway, and I don't think I've ever seen a dude go inside that house, not that I've been watching."

"Pfft. Creeper," I snort at him.

"Hey, I'm a man of opportunity." He quirks his head back.

"Well, this is certainly an opportunity." I scan over her face. In the picture, her dark hair is pulled back in a ponytail. Her milky white skin is dotted with a smattering of light freckles. She has full, kissable lips and the most amazing large chocolate eyes. The white tank top she's wearing is tight and low-cut enough that there are several inches of cleavage peeking up out of the top. *Yummy.*

"Scan through the pictures." Devlin leans over so that he can see the phone too, and I put it between us to scroll through the five available photos.

All of them are selfies, and there isn't an unattractive one in the bunch.

I had known she was pretty from seeing her from afar, but I had always assumed she had a boyfriend. Girls like her usually do. The ones with beautiful smiles, amazing curves, and ample breasts. Even if she doesn't have a boyfriend, though, I doubt she's after what we want.

I frown and tap the button to close the app.

Devlin's mouth drops open as he stares at me in disbelief. "What in the hell, man?"

"Dude, she's our neighbor." I give him an incredulous look.

"So?"

"So it would be awkward if we Liked her."

"What are you talking about? She obviously likes one of us. You caught her staring out the window at us." He gestures towards next door.

"One of us. Not both of us," I remind him.

"How do you know? Are you some mind reader?" He snatches the phone from me to pull the app back up, but it has already re-loaded and is displaying someone else's picture. He couldn't scowl deeper if he tried. "Look what you did." He tosses the phone onto my lap.

"Yes, look what I did. I saved us from embarrassing ourselves." I roll my eyes at him.

He stands, towering over me. "Get up and put on some pants."

"Why?" I arch an eyebrow at him.

"Because we're going over there. Right now." He places his hands on his hips as if to show me he means business.

"Are you out of your mind?" I rake my fingers through my hair, a small laugh escaping my lips.

"Hardly. If you think I'm spending Friday night sitting on this couch with you, you're out of *your* mind. Besides, we already know she's at home. We might as well take the opportunity while it's there." His eyes shift to the front door.

"Were you even listening to what I just said." My fingers curl around the couch cushion, lazily cementing me in place.

He rolls his wrist absentmindedly. "Neighbor. Awkward. Blah, blah, blah. Seriously, though, what's the worst that could happen?"

She could say no. Then what? It's not like we're close or even know each other at this point. She rarely comes out of her house except for when she's going somewhere. The times we see her are few and far between.

I sigh in disbelief that I'm actually starting to cave. This is a stupid idea, but one never knows what could happen if they don't try.

"So what's your big plan?" I deflate as if I still want to resist. The thought of talking to the foxy-looking brunette is starting to get my blood boiling, though.

"We play it by ear." He sounds so carefree and confident that it takes some of my fear of rejection away.

"That's hardly a plan."

"Come on." He nods towards the door. "I've got this.

You don't even have to say anything. Just follow my lead."

I inhale deeply, my heart beating faster from all of the unknown possibilities. "Fine. Let me put some pants on."

CHAPTER THREE
ROSE

Dishes. Lovely dishes.

It's amazing how they can pile up when you live alone. You'd think that with only yourself to look after, it would make keeping the kitchen clean a lot easier. The truth of the matter, though, is that when you rarely have house guests, it tends to make you lazier. At least, in my case it does.

I'm about ten minutes into scrubbing a week's worth of dishes, my mind going over all of the crappy dates I've been on in the recent past. I know that dating is a numbers game, but I'm really beginning to wonder if there is someone out there for me. I've gone out with at least a dozen guys since I got back into the dating scene. The majority of them were duds. The few that weren't never called me back. It makes me question if something is wrong with me, which is depressing.

I've always thought I was one of the better female fish in the sea. Sure, I'm not super model gorgeous, but I own my own home, my car is paid off, I have a great career and I'm not a gold digger. Maybe a lot of guys are intimidated by a girl who can take care of herself. I don't know anymore.

The doorbell rings, and I let out a deep sigh. With only two dishes left to wash, it's a bit irritating to be drawn away from the task.

For half a second, I think about not answering the door, but then I remember that I'm expecting a delivery. I ordered a projector last week to convert my living room into a home theater. While the package doesn't need to be signed for, the idea of leaving such an expensive item on my front porch for whoever walks by to steal isn't very appealing.

I dry my hands on a dishtowel before sauntering to the front door. I look like absolute crap in a pair of baggy sweatpants, a black tank top with bleach stains on it(it's my cleaning tank top) and my favorite blown-out bra. My hair is tied into a bun with about as much care as I took to get dressed. Even though the delivery man probably isn't cute, I really don't want him—or anyone, for that matter—seeing me like this. If I take my time getting to the door, he'll probably be gone when I open it. That's how those guys operate around here. Set your package on your doorstep, ring the doorbell and disappear into the sunset to make their next delivery.

I press my palms against the door and lean in to gaze out the peephole and make sure that the delivery man is gone before I open the door. It's not the delivery man though. And as my eyes focus on the two men standing on the other side of the door, my chest grows tight with a mix of excitement and stress.

"Holy shit," I whisper before jumping away from the door and clamping my hand over my mouth.

In an instant, my nerves are shot.

Should I open the door? I can't looking like this. But there's no time to change.

I peek out the peephole again. My neighbors look like they're getting bored with waiting. If I don't go out there soon, they'll leave and I may not get another opportunity to talk to them.

Throwing sanity to the wind, I unbolt the door. This is not the way to make a good first impression, looking like a rag doll that's been thrown from the back of a truck and run over several times. What does it really matter, though? They're just my neighbors.

"Hello," my voice comes out low and annoyed, and I cringe internally from the sound of it. Why did I say it like that?

My brunette neighbor opens his mouth to speak, but then he stops and gives me a panty melting grin. A shiver rocks me to my core, and my knees suddenly feel weak. Blondie is behind him looking stoic, but that's sexy too. My body temperature rises about ten degrees just from looking at them.

"I'm sorry. Did we catch you at a bad time? We can come back later." Mr. Brunette points behind himself, half-turned as if he's ready to leave.

My self-confidence takes a nosedive. Do I look so horrible that they already want to run away?

I push a stray strand of hair behind my ear. "No. It's fine. I was just doing dishes. Um, what do you need?"

Blondie wrinkles his nose and scratches the back of his neck, seeming like he wants to leave as well. This could not be any more awkward if it were orchestrated.

"My friend and I just wanted to come over and introduce ourselves, since we're new to the neighborhood and all." Mr. Brunette glances back at Blondie before returning his attention to me. "My name is Devlin and this is Gareth." He extends his hand to me.

My gaze falls to Devlin's hand as if the gesture is foreign to me. Then my brain catches up and I move to shake it. "Hi. I'm Rose. Nice to meet you."

"Rose. That's a pretty name." Devlin flashes me another charming smile before stepping aside to let Gareth shake my hand.

Just touching them makes my nipples bead. I glance

down at my chest and my cheeks heat up like someone splashed coffee in my face. I want to run away and hide, but that would be too strange. Surely, this interaction won't last very long. I can get through it. I have to.

As if reading my mind, Gareth's eyes falls to my chest. They only linger there for a moment, but I still caught him looking—noticing my body's reaction. My face feels feverish from all of the blushing I'm doing.

"It's nice to meet you both," I manage to choke out before withdrawing back into the house and crossing my arms over my chest.

"So." Devlin clasps his hands together in front of him. "I'm just going to cut to the chase and say that we noticed your picture on this dating app we're using. That was you, wasn't it?"

My mouth drops open in disbelief that he's bringing that up. For a moment, I think about lying, but I am kind of curious to see where he's going with this.

I swallow the hard lump that has formed in the back of my throat before speaking. "Yeah, that's me. I'm...single." It sounds more like a question than a statement.

"So are we." Devlin gestures between him and Gareth. "What a coincidence."

I eye them both suspiciously, deciding to be bold. "I saw you guys on the app too, but I couldn't figure out who the profile was for. You're both in all of the pictures."

"Oh, it's for both of us," he replies as if that's normal.

I shift my weight, my brow creasing as my confusion deepens. "You know, the app is free, so you could both have your own separate accounts."

Devlin stares at me blankly for a moment. Then his expression cracks with amusement. "It's a joint account. For both of us. Since we're both looking."

I close my eyes and shake my head. Wow, this guy is dense. Apparently, he has no idea how the online dating game works.

"We're into polyamory," Gareth chimes in.

"Oh." A light bulb goes off inside of my head as it all comes together. Then I have to refrain from looking shocked. "Oh."

"Yeah." Devlin nods. "We like to share women."

"Oh." I try to regain my composure but fall flat. "Good for you," is all I can come up with.

Apparently, my reaction wasn't good enough. They look like they expect something more. I'm not sure where to go with this. Right now they're reminding me of a Craigslist ad, the creepy kind where you open it up and see dick pics. Did they come over to ask me for a threesome?

"So you guys are bi?" I point at them, struggling to make conversation. What a weird thing to talk about the first time you meet someone.

"No." Devlin shakes his head. "Gareth and I are close but not that close," he laughs. "We just like being involved with the same woman. You see, I'm in the military, which makes it hard to carry out a normal relationship since I get deployed every so often. Gareth tends to work long hours at the hospital. With the way our schedules are, it's hard to keep a woman happy when we date separately. Together, though, it works.

"Plus, it's like a bonus for the woman. Two loving men. We're both financially stable and emotionally available. The woman we're with wants for nothing."

It does sound like a pretty sweet deal. They're both stupidly gorgeous. One is in the military, the other in the medical field. It's like a fetish fantasy times two. Still, if something sounds too good to be true, it usually is.

"Um." I look around nervously, feeling trapped.

"I suppose you're wondering why I'm even telling you all of this." Devlin glances down at his feet for a moment before his eyes meet mine.

"Kinda." I screw my face.

"Well." He rocks on his heels. "We saw your picture on the dating site. You're single. We're single. So I figured it wouldn't hurt to come over here and express interest."

Express interest. Really? They're actually interested in me. Both of them?

"This is a lot to take in." I rub the back of my neck.

"Too much for you?" Devlin quirks an eyebrow, looking cocky.

I roll my eyes, remembering their profile name. "Really?" I place a hand on my hip and tilt my head to the side.

"Sorry. Had to," he laughs but then quickly regains his composure. "How about this? Come over for dinner tonight. No strings attached. Say eightish? We'll cook for you. Gareth makes a mean steak. That is if you're not a vegetarian." He cringes slightly as if he fears he made a mistake.

"I'm not a vegetarian." I giggle.

He pulls his phone out of his pocket to check the time. "Awesome. Um, there's still some time between now and eight. I know this is all really sudden, so if you need to take some time to think about it, that's fine. If you don't find us attractive or aren't interested or don't think this is for you, then you don't have to show up. No hard feelings." Devlin holds his hands up and takes a step back.

"Alright." I stare at him, still processing the offer.

"Hopefully, we'll see you later." He gives Gareth a gentle slap on the shoulder to get him moving.

"We'll see."

"Bye." Gareth waves at me awkwardly before they both turn away and head back towards their house.

I stand there for several seconds watching them walk away while I slowly close the door. My eyes drift down to their butts. Devlin is in dark jeans and Gareth is wearing cut off shorts. I bet they both look amazing naked. I've already seen half of the package, and I can't deny that I want to see the rest. Still, this is absolutely insane.

It's not until I close the door that I realize how rapidly my heart is beating. That entire conversation was incredibly surreal. Part of me doesn't even believe it happened.

They came over not to introduce themselves but to hit on me. That's the real reason why they showed up. The thought makes my heart flutter.

Two handsome men vying for my attention. Not vying. Sharing?

How does that even work, I wonder.

I exhale a long breath and go into my office to get on the computer. Gareth said that they're into polyamory, but I don't know much about it. The first thing that comes to mind is polygamy, specifically the shows on television where one guy has ten wives. Sister wives, I think they're called. However, Devlin said that they want to share one woman, not the other way around.

From all of my research, it seems that polyamory is a loving relationship between multiple people. Does that mean that Devlin and Gareth love each other? It's still all a bit confusing to me. Maybe I'll ask more questions if I go over tonight.

But that brings up the real question. Should I go over?

I just met these guys, and I've learned from enough bad dates that it's never a good idea to go into the home of a strange guy when you don't know his intentions. Two men could be double trouble.

Double trouble.

A smirk crosses my face as I think of what that trouble that could be. One sucking on my nipples while the other rams his thick cock into me. Or maybe me on my hands and knees, sucking one of them off while the other takes me from behind. Just imaging the three of us writhing naked together on a bed is getting me all worked up. Their hands on me, groping me roughly. Their mouths kissing me. They're dicks fighting to get inside of me.

No. I shake my head. I can't think like that. Meaningless sex will only make me feel horrible about myself. I've had the one-night stand experience, and it wasn't good. I don't want that again.

Going over there could be nothing but bad news. Another mistake.

I sigh, lifting my hand to look at my watch. As Devlin said, there's still plenty of time to decide.

CHAPTER FOUR
DEVLIN

"That went well." I lounge back on the sofa, pleased.

"You really think so?" Gareth huffs.

"I do." I nod, a smirk creeping across my face as I think of how disheveled Rose looked. I can't help but wonder if she has any idea how sexy she is. Everything in me wanted to pull her hair out of that bun, watch it cascade over her shoulders, press her against the door and take her right there. Who cares if the whole neighborhood saw? It would be hot as hell.

"You have high hopes, man." Gareth is already in the kitchen getting everything prepared for dinner. He looks nervous, but he has no reason to be. I saw the flash of desire in Rose's eyes. She wanted him. She wanted us both.

"What makes you say that?" I flip on the television, catching the tail end of the game I was watching earlier.

"She looked freaked out," stress is apparent in his voice.

"You worry too much." I roll my eyes at him even though he can't see it. He's always been the pessimist between us, constantly anticipating the worst case scenario.

"I'm just telling you what I saw." He pulls a bag of new

potatoes out of the pantry and gets to work peeling them.

"Did you see that her nipples were hard?"

That shuts him up. I know he was looking. How could he not have been. She's got the most perfect set of tits ever.

"She was also blushing," I add.

"She could have just been hot," he mutters.

"Hot for our cocks," I snort.

"So vulgar. I thought we weren't about that."

"We're not." I don't even look at him. "But I'm keeping it real. I want to bury my dick in her. Bury my dick in her while you bury your dick in her." I smirk at him. "Fill her so full that all she can do is moan in pleasure. See that pretty, little mouth in a permanent O."

"She does have nice breasts. And a pretty face. I hope she comes tonight." He nods while he works.

"Oh, she'll come. Again and again and again if we have anything to do with it."

"What happened to no strings attached?" Gareth quirks an eyebrow at me though he's grinning all the while.

"You know I'm just playing." I yawn. "We wouldn't want to scare her away. She is our neighbor, after all. If she's not up for what we have to offer, then that will be the end of it."

"And we'll know that if she comes over or not." His eyes widen for effect.

"Even if she comes over, it doesn't mean anything. Girls are flighty. Besides, we have no idea what her personality is like." I screw my face.

That has been an issue in the past. Some of the hottest girls are as dumb as a box of rocks. That hasn't kept me from fucking them, but it has definitely kept me from pursuing a relationship with them. Thankfully, Gareth and I have the same taste when it comes to intelligence. It's brains or get the fuck out.

"Her personality is awkward. But I think it's kind of cute. Hopefully, she loosens up a bit when she's over."

"That's what wine is for." I wait for a commercial before pulling myself off of the sofa to rummage through our wine cabinet. "What should we go with tonight?"

"I'm thinking a merlot or cabernet sauvignon. It will pair well with the steaks." Gareth glances at me over the kitchen island.

"How about the Harlan Estate, Cabernet Sauvignon Double Magnum 2009?" I pull the bottle out and look at the label. "Double Magnum, like us," I laugh.

"This is a first date. We're not marrying the girl. Get the Robert Mondavi, Cabernet Sauvignon Reserve."

"You're so cheap." I shake my head at him, putting the first bottle away to grab the less expensive one.

"We don't even know if she likes red wine." He empties the bowl of potato peelings into the trash.

"I like red wine." I stand with the bottle.

"Well, if you're being selfish, then get whatever bottle you want. You shouldn't choose one just because it makes your dick sound bigger." He smirks.

I pretend to throw something at him, and he ducks, reminding me of a dog chasing after an imaginary ball. "I have nothing." I hold up my free hand and chuckle at him.

"You're a dick." He glowers at me. "Are you going to help me with this or not? This dinner was your idea, after all."

"I am helping. I got the wine." I place the bottle on the kitchen counter. He's not amused. "Fine, fine. I'll go start the grill."

"Please do. I don't want her thinking that I'm the bitch of this relationship."

"But you are the bitch of the relationship." I smile at him over my shoulder as I head to the backyard to fire up the grill.

It takes a while for my confidence to begin to falter. The more I replay the conversation with Rose over in my head, the more I worry that she won't show up. Gareth was right, she did seem a bit uncomfortable. And I did come on way too strong. Only time will tell, though, and we're no worse off than when we started if she doesn't show up. Still, I hope she does come. Gareth and I have been alone for far too long.

I try not to think about it as I help Gareth set up for dinner. The mood shifts while we work. There's less ball busting and a lot more reflecting on the possible scenarios. If Rose doesn't show up tonight, we'll both be depressed. I imagine that we'll just eat dinner and then go out to a bar. If she does show up, though...who knows what the night will hold.

The clock ticks down to eight o'clock. With all the preparations done, Gareth and I sit on the sofa. Waiting.

The air is heavy as the minutes pass. 8:00 PM comes and goes, and a sick feeling balls in my stomach as the reality hits me that Rose might not come. At 8:10 PM, Gareth finally turns to me. "Should we eat?"

My mouth is dry and there's a hollowness in my chest. I had really hoped this would work out. Instead, we just ended up making asses of ourselves. Gareth was right. We never should have gone over there.

"Are you hungry?" I glance at him.

He sighs. "Not really, but we should eat. I see a whole lot of alcohol in our future tonight."

"Alcohol and a one-night stand." I force a grin.

"I'm whatever at this point." He pushes himself off of the sofa.

I feel bad, like this was a bigger let down for him than it was for me. Of course, I'm disappointed too. But he has talked a whole lot about being lonely lately. I'm not sure how much longer this can go on before he surrenders to the idea of trying to find someone on his own. And we both know how that always turns out.

"You made the right call on the Robert Mondavi, Cabernet Sauvignon Reserve." I stand to go to the kitchen to find a corkscrew.

When I'm halfway there, the doorbell rings. I quickly

pull my phone out of my pocket to check the time. The display reads 8:13 PM. Still, I know it's her. Who else could it be?

I turn to look at Gareth.

He lets out a breathy laugh. "Maybe we weren't stood up after all."

"There's only one way to find out." I half-walk, half-jog to the door. Before I open it, I plaster on my best confident smile. No hint of the doubt I had before is left on my face.

Rose is standing there, looking sheepish and beautiful. Her dark hair is pulled back into a sleek ponytail. She's wearing a simple blue and white dress, but it's absolutely stunning on her, hugging all of her curves perfectly.

"Sorry I'm late." She holds her clutch in front of her, her voice mousey.

"We were starting to worry you weren't going to show up," Gareth calls over my shoulder.

"Come in." I step aside, ushering her in. As soon as her back is to me, my grin turns wolfish. The night is just about to begin.

CHAPTER FIVE
ROSE

Delicious food, great wine, and devastatingly handsome men. What more could a girl want? Much more. More than she should. Desires completely fueled by the headiness of wine. Maybe not completely fueled, but the alcohol certainly didn't help to tame what was already there.

It's amazing how quickly awkwardness turned to comfort after a few glasses of red. For the most part, the guys have kept things casual. Over dinner, we talked about our jobs and backgrounds and all of the standard get-to-know-you stuff. Now the meal is over and I'm sandwiched between them on the sofa. And by sandwiched, I mean they're both sitting so close to me that I don't even have to put effort into keeping my legs shut. This should feel weird, but somehow it doesn't.

There's a Vampire Diaries marathon playing on the television, and I can't help but wear a shit-eating grin. Either they're bisexual or they're watching this to please me. I'm going to take a guess that it's the latter of the two. Devlin acts far too manly to be into a show like this. Gareth seems more passive, going with the flow.

If they're trying to impress me, the cooking and being

gentlemen has done it. This is overkill. I probably just think that because I don't really like The Vampire Diaries, though. Since I'm not able to concentrate on the show due to lack of interest, it seems like all of the chemistry in the room has dried up. Now we're just sitting around, and nervousness is beginning to creep back in. I feel like I need to do something to keep it from turning into full-blown awkwardness.

"So, are you guys sure you're not bisexual because I'm pretty sure no straight guy would watch this." I swirl the wine in my glass before taking another sip. This is glass number two, and it's definitely helped to remove some of the filter between my mouth and my brain. I'm not so sure that's a good thing. Hopefully, I don't say something too offensive or stupid. That does seem to happen from time to time when I've been drinking.

"I promise we're not." Devlin reassures me.

"Because if I read correctly, polyamory is a loving relationship between all people, which would have to mean that you two love each other." I set my glass down on the coffee table, realizing I've had enough. My face flapping could potentially ruin this for me if I drink anymore.

"We do love each other." Devlin looks across me at Gareth. "Like best friends love each other. But we don't fuck each other."

That's too bad. It would be kinda hot if you did. I think it, but I dare not say it. I would not want them thinking that I'm weird or some pervert.

"I don't get how that works. So like, does one of you watch while the other...does his thing?" I gesture between them.

Devlin pushes himself away from the sofa slightly, leaning towards me. His smirk is absolutely devilish, making my pulse race as he crosses my personal space boundary. "Would you like for us to show you?"

I'm so shocked by how suddenly the mood in the room has shifted that I feel paralyzed. I'm not afraid, more nervous. In the beat of a hummingbird's wings, things have gone from casual to sexual. Devlin looks like a predator eying prey, and I'm right in his crosshairs.

My heart thumps in my chest as his face draws near to mine. With Gareth sitting so close to me, there's nowhere to escape to. This is exactly why I was reluctant to come over in the first place.

Before Devlin's mouth has a chance to make contact with mine, I raise my hand, creating a barrier between us. "I don't do one-night stands."

He looks somewhat disappointed but doesn't pressure me further, resting back on the sofa. "Neither do we."

The playful atmosphere I was trying to create dissipates, and we're all seriousness. You couldn't cut the tension in the room with a knife. Part of me wants to leave, but a bigger part of me is stubborn. If I walk away now, I might be throwing away a great opportunity. An opportunity for what, though?

"What would this be if not a one-night stand?" It feels like I'm just asking to be lied to. This is where they ply me with slick words. Say everything that needs to be said to get me into bed. Guys are good at that. It's like a game to them. And I bet that both Devlin and Gareth are great players.

"We'd like a relationship, if things go well," Gareth says, staring forward as if he's afraid to look at me.

I'm surprised to hear him speak first. He's the strong, silent type. Shy and fairly reserved in comparison to his friend. Just from the way he acts, I'm inclined to believe that he's the most honest of the two as well.

"It would actually be pretty convenient, if you think about it." Devlin stretches and slips his arm around me. "I mean, you live right next door. We could see each other whenever we wanted to. It's not like distance would be an issue.

"Gareth likes cooking, so you could come over for dinner several times a week. Or we could cook at your place. Do you like cooking?" He glances down at me.

"Not particularly." I feel almost bad admitting it, but cooking has never been my forte.

"No matter." He shrugs it off. "We're both pretty handy around the house, so if you need anything fixed, we could help you with that. And you've probably already noticed, but we both know a lot about cars, so if you ever have problems with yours, we could come take a look. If one of us doesn't know how to fix something, the other usually does."

I can't help but grin. He sounds like a salesman. As if the fact that they're both gorgeous and sweet isn't enough of a selling point.

"Dual MacGyvers." I nod.

"We can snake your pipes and make sure your engine purrs like a kitten." Devlin waggles his eyebrows at me.

"You did not just say that." Gareth hides his face behind his hands, and I laugh. If not for his adorable reaction, it might have been a completely awkward and uncomfortable moment. I'm getting the feeling that Gareth keeps Devlin in check. They seem good together. How would they be if I were thrown into the mix?

I silently chastise myself for even considering it. There's an internal push and pull. Should I stay or should I go? This is all a bit overwhelming. Never in my entire life have I considered a three-way relationship with two men.

Devlin curls his fingers into my hair and I shiver. When I glance over at him, the predatory gaze has returned.

"Sex doesn't have to happen tonight, right?" I arch an eyebrow at him.

"Of course not. No strings attached, remember," his tone is casual, but his expression doesn't change. The way he's looking at me stirs something deep inside of me—makes my thighs press together. "We can take things as slow as you want. Or as fast." He squeezes his eyes together. Not quite a wink, but definitely a mischievous look.

"What he's trying to say is," Gareth chimes in, stealing my attention, "we think that you're smart, beautiful, funny. We want to be with you. We'd like to see if we can make this work."

"Mhm," my voice is clipped, my nervousness shining through.

Things seem a bit too intense. I'm starting to feel cornered. And while I do want to mull over what they're offering, I don't feel like I can do it when they're both so close.

Abruptly, I stand, feeling oxygen and cool air rush in from no longer being wedged between two warm bodies. I turn to them, and they both look up at me as if expecting an answer to a question that was never asked.

"I'll be right back. I need to use the restroom."

"Our house is your house." Devlin gestures towards the bathroom.

I nod before hurriedly making my way to the restroom and locking myself inside. Safely away from them, I feel like I can think again. I stare at my reflection in the mirror, wondering what in the hell I got myself into.

Earlier today, I was fantasizing about these two men. They both want me. I should be elated, but somehow I'm so unsure.

I take a deep breath and shake it out. "Get it together, Rose. Just because they're gorgeous and willing and you're horny doesn't mean you have to jump into bed with them tonight. If this is really what they want—what you want—then it's worth waiting and taking the time to get to know each other.

"You'll go out there, thank them for the lovely evening and leave. Then in the coming days, you'll see what happens. If this is real—if it's meant to be—things will fall into place. If it's not, then they'll fizzle out. You've got this. Just stick to your guns and everything will be alright."

I hold my head up high, my confidence solidified. It is time to make my escape. I've lingered long enough and if I stay any longer, there's only one way things can go, and I definitely don't want that.

With new resolve, I wash my hands and walk out of the bathroom with my game plan cemented in my mind. As soon as my eyes land on Gareth standing by the sofa without a shirt on, though, my brain gets completely scrambled. At that moment, I know I've lost to lust. If either one of them hits on me again, anything goes.

CHAPTER SIX
GARETH

"Things are going well though you could lay off of the creeping a bit. I think you're scaring her away." I wait until Rose is the bathroom with the door closed before I speak. I gaze across the empty space at Devlin. He's still sitting with his arm lounged across the back of the sofa, looking pleased with himself as usual.

"They are going well. I think she might be the one." His eyes stay fixed on the bathroom door.

"I think so too." I nod, glancing down at my lap. My cock is rock hard, straining against my cutoffs. I've had an erection ever since the three of us came to sit together on the sofa—ever since I felt Rose's warm, milky white thigh press against mine. How could I not get turned on by being so close to such an amazing creature?

When she first came over, I was afraid that things would quickly fizzle out. She seemed timid, like she was entering into enemy territory. Devlin immediately poured her a glass of wine, though, and by the time she was halfway through it, we were all talking and laughing like we'd known each other for years. Everything just fell into place—felt so right. Since then, I've been obsessing over her smile, loving the sound of her laughter, watching her eyes shimmer. Of course, I've been noticing other parts of her too. The way her chest rises and falls when she breathes, the sway of her hips when she walks. I want her so badly that it almost hurts, but I know not to press her boundaries. More than anything, I don't want to scare her away. Devlin is taking a more aggressive approach.

"We can't fuck this up," I tell him.

"We're not going to." He doesn't even look at me.

"What you're thinking is going to happen tonight is not going to happen." I raise an eyebrow at him in warning.

"Oh, yes it is. She's so close to caving." A toothy grin spreads across his face.

"You're reading this wrong," I sigh.

"I'm not. Trust me. I've got a plan." His gaze finally leaves the door, and he leans forward to grab my nearly empty glass of wine from the coffee table.

"What plan?" I give him a quizzical look.

Without another word, he dumps the contents of the glass onto the front of my shirt.

I'm on my feet in an instant, my temper flaring. "What in the hell, man?"

"Take your shirt off." Devlin quickly sets the glass back down.

The door to the bathroom opens, and I feel confused, rushed and a bit panicked.

Devlin shoots back into his seat like he never moved at all. He looks up at me, eyes wide while he mouths the words again. I'm not sure what his game plan is, but I decide to follow it, pulling my shirt off and tossing it onto the arm of the sofa before checking my chest to see how much of the wine seeped through onto my skin.

Rose walks out of the bathroom and pauses for a moment, standing there staring at me with a blank expression.

"Dude, you're such a klutz," Devlin chastises me before turning his attention to Rose. "Look at this guy, spilling wine all over himself."

It takes everything in me not to glare at him. He could have spilled wine on himself, but he didn't want to look clumsy. I'm not sure how he thinks that making me seem like a slob is going to charm Rose into wanting to be with us.

"Do you need a towel?" Her eyes shift toward the kitchen and her cheeks flush with color.

"Yeah, that would be great." Devlin smiles at her.

As she diverts to the kitchen to rummage through the drawers for a towel, I look down at Devlin, completely befuddled about what's going on. The question is in my eyes, but he doesn't answer me. He keeps his focus on Rose, watching her as she moves.

She returns with a dishtowel, holding it out to me. I reach to take it, but Devlin stands and intervenes. For several seconds, the moment seems forced, probably because it is. He takes her hand with the towel in it and pulls her forward, wiping down my chest.

Our eyes lock, and warmth and desire pulse through me. I fear that she'll look away, but she doesn't. Her cheeks are rosy pink, but her gaze goes dark with secret yearnings.

Devlin pulls the towel from her hand, then he presses her palm onto my bare skin, over my heart. I wonder if she can feel how fiercely it's beating. I'm nervous but confident. This was the trap all along. We have her right where we want her. Now it's my job to seal the deal. The pressure is on. If I mess this up, it's all over.

I place my hand on top of hers, and Devlin withdraws his. My gaze falls to the fullness of Rose's lips. They're parted slightly, ready for my kiss. How I want to kiss her.

I hold my breath and lean in, half expecting her to pull away. It's such a delicate situation. Devlin might feel certain that she wants this, but I'm not.

As if reading my fear, Rose jerks her head back a little. A ball of snakes wind in my stomach, spitting their poison and filling me with the bile of reject. She turns and looks at Devlin. I watch him in my peripheral vision, trying to see their exchange. He simply nods. Then she returns her attention to me, and I know that the opportunity isn't lost.

I step in and slide a hand around the curvature of her hip, drawing her closer. Timidness returns to her eyes, but she doesn't pull away. When I lean in this time, there's no resistance. My lips meet hers, tasting their sweetness, and I know that we've won.

CHAPTER SEVEN
ROSE

What am I doing?

This is exactly what I said I wouldn't do. It's too late now though. My hormones bowled me over the second I stepped out of the bathroom and saw Gareth standing there shirtless. He looked like something from my own personal fantasy collection. Maybe because he is. I've pleasured myself to thoughts of being with him—thoughts of being with both of them—before.

Now here they are looking dreamy. Here we all are. And the alcohol has gone straight to my vagina. Past my head, melting me into a puddle of wanton desire.

Maybe I could have held my resolve if I hadn't touched him. But the second that my hand felt the wall of hard muscle beneath the towel...that was the end of me. Or was it when Devlin took the towel away? Or maybe it was the way that Gareth looked at me. His expression was so earnest, so full of adoration. I don't think it matters anymore. When he kissed me, it was over.

And now I'm lost in his lips. In the feel of his hands on my body. In the headiness of his cologne. In knowing that Devlin is standing only a few feet away and I'm going to get to kiss him too.

This is so wrong, but I can't stop it. Even if they're just playing me and I end up emotionally destroyed afterward, I want to feel this—want to know what it's like to be with two beautiful men at the same time.

Can I even handle both of them at once? I guess I'm about to find out.

Gareth's mouth is hot against mine. He's holding me like he doesn't want to let me go—like he doesn't want to share.

I slide a hand around the back of his neck, my fingertips gliding into the hair at his nape while I stand on tiptoe to deepen the kiss. He tastes like wine and trouble. I don't care anymore though. I want trouble. Double trouble.

Devlin steps up to cage me between them. He brushes my hair away from my neck and kisses me there, sending a shiver of pleasure coursing through my body. I moan softly into Gareth's mouth only seconds before I feel Devlin's hand on my cheek, turning my head so that I can kiss him as well.

I reciprocate fully, smirking slightly at the differences in the way that they kiss. Gareth's lips were sweet and accommodating, passionate but gentle. Devlin is all aggression. His tongue darts into my mouth, battling for space. Touching and teasing and claiming.

Gareth boldly cups my breasts, and my nipples turn into rocks. His face dips to my cleavage, his tongue trailing a path there. I tilt my head and press back against Devlin's dick to feel it grow. He's big, and I can't wait to have him inside of me. Can't wait to have both of them inside of me.

I nip at Devlin's bottom lip, giving it a gentle tug before pulling away from the kiss. "Should we take this to the bedroom?"

"But I'm having so much fun right here." Devlin slides his hand down the front of my dress, gripping the hem and hiking it up.

I purse my lips, wanting to pout until I feel his fingers creeping up my thigh towards my underwear. Gareth caresses my cheek, stealing my attention. He leans in to kiss me again, and I acquiesce.

My body is on fire from sensation. My core is so hot that I'm worried I might burn Devlin when his hand finally reaches it.

He slips his fingers beneath my panties, brushing softly across the strip of hair on my mound. I tense up for a moment, thinking about how fast everything is moving. This was completely unexpected. Or maybe it wasn't. Perhaps I had secretly hoped it would happen all along. Still, there's the tiniest bit of hesitation, but I'm beyond the point where it matters anymore. There's no going back.

Gareth's hands reach around me to unzip the back of my dress. It's such a smooth move, I hardly even realize it's happening since his lips never leave mine. When I open my eyes, the look he's giving me is strangely soothing, and I feel like everything will be okay if I let them do this— that I can trust them with my body.

Devlin backs off for a moment to slide my dress down my body. Part of me is discontent that he didn't touch me more, but I know it's coming. They're both too aroused to stop now. And so am I.

I feel like a doll, standing there while they undress me the rest of the way. Gareth slips my panties down over my hips while Devlin unclasps my bra. And then I'm naked. Naked and vulnerable with two of the most handsome men I've ever seen.

"This is hardly fair," I purr as they cage me in again, their hands wandering everywhere, making my skin prickle.

"I think it's plenty fair," Devlin whispers over my shoulder.

"I'm completely naked, and you boys are both mostly clothed." I reach around to caress his face, dragging my fingers across the thin layer of stubble on his jaw.

"We can change that." Devlin quickly pulls his shirt off

to please me.

"We should take this to the bedroom." Gareth nods towards the master bedroom.

"I agree." I trace a path down the middle of his chest with my index finger. Down, down it goes, following the valley of his stomach until it reaches his belt. His cock is straining hard against his shorts. I can't wait for him to take them off so that I can see it. My mouth is already salivating at the thought of sucking him off.

"As the lady wishes." Devlin turns to walk away, and Gareth offers me his hand, following Devlin into the master bedroom.

Each step I take makes my heart beat faster. I knew there was no going back when I allowed them to get me naked, but being in the bedroom with them adds another layer of realness to this. They're both going to fuck me, and this is going to be a night that I'll never forget for the rest of my life.

Gareth leads me to the bed, and I sit down on the side of it, my eyes flitting to Devlin while he takes off his pants. Need races through me as they peel their clothes off until they're both naked, cocks fully erect and impressive. So much hard muscle and firm length and deliciousness.

"Come here," I beckon to them, holding my hands out to my sides. I want to wrap my arms around them, kiss their stomachs, suck their dicks. It's so dirty and wrong, but I want it so badly.

Gareth comes to me, but Devlin bends slightly to grab my legs, putting them up on the bed and climbing up behind me. I follow through with my plan, wrapping my hand around Gareth's ass. He feels so solid, like he's chiseled out of stone. My eyes stay fixed on his manhood, my mouth ravenous for him. I pull him to me, my tongue flicking out to tease the tip of his cock. He hisses in pleasure, his eyes hooded with lust.

"Fuck, you're so hot," Devlin tells me. "If we had known you'd be like this, we would have come over the day that we moved in." He slides his hands between my thighs and pries them open, making me bow my legs. "I want to taste you so badly."

A blush creeps across my cheeks at how exposed I am, but all modesty was out the window long ago. This is me in my most primal state, ready to be fucked.

I drag the blade of my tongue up and down Gareth's shaft. He tastes clean, like soap and skin and sex.

His hand crawls down my collarbone, then further to grope one of my breasts. He pinches my nipple, and an electric shock fires all the way down to my core. I latch my lips around him and suck hard, and he groans in abandonment, sweet music to my ears.

Devlin pulls me roughly to him, and I feel the heat of his breath dance over my clit, making it throb to life. The sensation is followed by the wetness of his tongue darting out to stroke my nub. For a second, I think I'm going to climax on contact, but I somehow manage to hold myself together.

"Oh shit," I pant around Gareth's cock as Devlin licks down my slit.

He pulls apart my folds, making sure he has access to everything. His tongue is skilled and thorough, dancing around my cleft and vibrating there before sliding down into my wetness. It takes everything in me not to writhe against his face. I fist my hand into his dark locks, curling my fingers but not tugging. As if he knows what I want, he goes deeper, wraps his lips around my clit and applies pressure while his tongue taps my pleasure button.

"Oh," I whimper as an uncontrollable wave of pleasure crashes down on me.

Devlin pushes two fingers into me, thrusting them all the way to the knuckle, and I shatter completely, my pussy clamping around them.

Holy fuck.

I moan, my lips a paralyzed mess on Gareth's cock. He takes control, thrusting in and out of my mouth while I pant and my pussy contracts and Devlin prolongs my pleasure with the slick sweetness of his tongue. It's almost more than I can bear, and I feel kind of guilty that I'm not able to give as much as I'm receiving. If this is really what they want, though, then it's completely amazing. A girl could get used to this.

As soon as my orgasm ebbs, Devlin redirects his focus to my breasts, his hands kneading into them, his fingertips pinching and tweaking my nipples. I loll my tongue out, lost in the bliss of having so much attention. Even though I just climaxed, my clit is still pulsing and throbbing as if it's already gearing up again. I can't believe how alive my body feels from being with them. It's like an endless flow of sexual energy coursing between the three of us.

Gareth pulls his dick out of my mouth, and I'm left feeling empty. I gaze up at him, wanting more—wanting both of them inside of me.

Devlin sits on the side of the bed and pats his lap. "Come here."

A giggle escapes my lips as I crawl to him. I feel stupidly happy being with them, almost drunk from everything going on.

Gareth helps me off of the bed, and then he grabs me by the hips, keeping me facing him as he backs me up towards Devlin. My cheeks heat up as I realize what the plan is. As soon as I'm close enough, Gareth hands me off to Devlin. I look behind me as Devlin slowly guides me down onto his phallus.

The second I feel it crest my folds, my body tenses. I reach forward and clutch onto Gareth's forearm, gazing up at him with parted lips as I feel the round fullness of Devlin's glans pressing into me. He's so thick and hot.

"Ah," I whimper from the euphoria of the slow intrusion. "Oh God."

"You're so sexy," Gareth tells me. "It's so hot watching you take Devlin's dick."

"It feels amazing." I slide back on him, swallowing him

up. The fullness is everything I needed.

Devlin keeps a hold of my hips as he begins thrusting up into me. My thighs burn from trying to keep a bit of distance between us so that he can move.

"Sit back on him." Gareth smirks, perhaps noticing my struggle.

"Yeah, come here." Devlin grips my waist, pulling me down until my thighs atrophy and I'm forced to put all of my weight on him.

I lean against his chest, hooking my arm around his neck and tilting my head back. I moan shamelessly as he bucks up into me, practically forgetting for a moment that Gareth is there.

He doesn't let me forget for long, though.

Warm wetness slicks across my clit, and I gasp, my attention immediately redirecting to that spot between my legs where everything comes together to create heaven. Gareth is bending over to taste our joined parts. It's so hot that I can barely stand it—feels so incredible.

"Oh my God. Oh shit." I pant, feeling the tension between my legs mount again as Devlin pumps up into me while Gareth teases my clit with his mouth.

"Are you going to come again? Are you going to come all over my dick?" Devlin whispers into my ear, his voice all breathy lust.

Gareth stands, and for the first time since I've met him, he looks wicked. "Beg for it."

"What?" My mouth falls open in shock.

"We're not going to let you come again unless you beg for it." Devlin gropes my breasts, pulling me back against him as he stills.

The world stops, the build of pleasure between my legs slowly receding. The bastards are in sync, and I know that neither one of them are going to move unless I give them what they want.

"You're both evil." I glare at Gareth.

"Are we now?" he laughs.

Two can play this game, I think, a devious grin creeping across my face as I decide to take matters into my own hands. Why should I let them have all of the fun.

I muster up all of my strength, plant my feet on the floor, and bounce on Devlin's cock like I'm going to break him. Within seconds, the tides are turned. His hands leave my breasts to grip the bed, and his breathing becomes ragged.

"Holy shit," he pants.

Gareth just stares at me for a moment, his expression somewhere between aroused and impressed. He lazily strokes himself while I fuck his friend. The whole time, I hold his gaze. It's a strangely intimate moment. Intense and surreal, like I can feel him inside of me too.

"Fuck, I'm going to come. You've got to stop." Devlin practically pushes me off of him. The fact that he broke his composure is amusing. I didn't even think it was possible.

"Get over here." Gareth roughly turns me around, not even waiting for Devlin to recover before he's bending me over the bed.

He thrusts inside of me with one rough motion, and I cry out in disbelief at how forceful he's being. Almost instantly, my core goes from zero to sixty on the pleasure scale. This is something I never expected from him, and I absolutely love it. He's supposed to be the sweet, quiet one, but he's showing no mercy now.

I hold on like my life depends on it as he pounds into me to the point that I'm about to lose my balance. The friction is quickly driving me to new heights, and I don't know how much longer I can hold on. I grunt and groan with each thrust, practically drooling as the sensation of his balls slapping against my pussy from the quick, hard thrusting threatens to make me climax again.

The bed shifts beside me, and Devlin comes into my peripheral vision. Within seconds, he's presenting his cock to me. I open my mouth like I'm hungry for it. With this one act, the fantasy will come full circle, being pounded from both sides.

He slides his length to the back of my throat, and I immediately feel blissfully full. Every time Gareth thrusts, it pushes me into Devlin, making me take him incredibly deep, triggering my gag reflex. I'm so overwhelmed with dick that tears spill out the corners of my eyes. But it's good. Oh so good. Everything I wanted and more.

I try to mumble my pleasure around Devlin's cock, but nothing comes out but a garble of indecipherable sounds. They're both being aggressive. Devlin's pre-juices leak into my mouth, making my throat sticky. The smell of man and sex is all around me. I'm overwhelmed and fulfilled and so amazingly content.

"I'm going to come so hard," Gareth says behind me. His voice is so sexy that just the sound of it throws me over the edge.

I whimper as the world shifts around me, blinding me with pleasure. My toes curl as my pussy squeezes around Gareth's dick, my clit firing off again and again. My body is on sensory overload, and I'm so busy focusing on all of it that I almost forget to breathe.

"You're so God damn tight," Gareth growls. He picks up the pace, slamming into me, drawing out my orgasm.

Devlin does the same, his cock pistoning in and out of my mouth. I know what's coming next, and I brace myself for it.

They both pull out and simultaneously blow their loads. I bow my head and inhale deeply as I feel warm wetness paint me, a canvas to their climax. All I can do is stay there on all fours, catching my breath and grinning to myself. I still can't believe I did this, but I'm glad that I did.

As the high of sex starts to wear off, I wonder what happens next. Do I take the walk of shame covered in the memory of our coupling? Will they let me shower first? But more importantly, will I ever hear from them again, or did I just get used.

I wait for instructions, afraid to move and get come on their bed. Not that it matters. Most of it got on me, but not all. Messy boys, they are.

"Let's take a shower." Gareth pulls out of me and slaps my ass.

"That sounds lovely." I crawl off of the bed and stand.

Devlin immediately goes to the master bathroom for a towel to clean me off with. He wipes me down and then hands me the towel to let me get anything that he missed. Meanwhile, Gareth disappears into the bathroom to start the shower.

Now that the sex is over, I feel kind of awkward. They're not acting strangely at all. It's me, allowing myself to get stuck in my own head.

Devlin escorts me into the bathroom, and the three of us slip into the shower together. We spend the next fifteen minutes bathing each other. Gareth scrubs down my body while Devlin shampoos my hair. It's a nice pampering after a hard fucking. Once more, I feel like I'm in heaven.

It's not until the shower is over that the awkwardness returns. I wrap a towel around myself and head into the living room to retrieve my clothes and get dressed, sighing as I pick my underwear up off of the floor. *It's definitely time for the walk of shame now.*

"What are you doing?" Devlin's arms wrap around me, startling me.

"I'm getting dressed," I reply as if it's obvious.

"No, you're not. You're staying the night with us...unless you have something more important to do." He kisses the base of my neck, making me swoon.

I curl my hand around his forearm, giving it a gentle squeeze. "No, I don't have anything more important to do."

Sleeping between them is strange. As much as I'm glad that they asked me to stay, I feel a little claustrophobic. Gareth spoons me from behind while Devlin falls asleep on his stomach about a foot away. Even though they're not fighting over who gets to cuddle me, I'm still not used to sharing a bed with more than one person. Hell, I'm used to sleeping alone. This is something else I could get used to, though, with time.

Thanks to being exhausted, I'm able to fall asleep quickly. The morning seems to come just as fast, though.

I blink awake to the lights streaming in through the blinds. It takes me a moment to remember where I am, but then everything comes back to me. Gareth rolled over in his sleep and is facing away from me. Devlin's back is pressed against my arm, and we're glued together with sweat. Somehow, I find it amusing. That quickly fades though when I realize that I feel trapped again. It's always weird sleeping with someone for the first time—waking up in their bed.

I want to get up, but I'm afraid of rousing them. I don't even know if they're morning people or not. Maybe they'll get mad if I wake them up.

I decide to just lie there for a while.

Thankfully, it doesn't take long for Gareth to stir. I pretend to be asleep as he rolls out of bed and leaves the room. Devlin doesn't so much as twitch, so I can only assume that he's a heavy sleeper.

Cautiously, I crawl out of bed and get dressed before going to find Gareth. He's in the kitchen making breakfast, apparently the chef of the two.

"Morning." He smiles at me over his shoulder as he cracks eggs into a skillet.

"Morning." I yawn and stretch before leaning against the kitchen island.

"How did you sleep?"

"Hard." I trace a circle in the marble with my fingertip.

"Me too. It's been a while since I've been so worn out," he laughs.

"Me too." I grin.

"I hope you enjoyed yourself last night. We both do. I also hope you like your eggs sunny side up." His eyes widen.

"I did and I do. But you don't have to feed me." My expression sulks as I begin to think that I probably overstayed my welcome.

"Of course, we do. We're not going to send our girl off hungry."

"Your girl, huh?" His cute little comment makes my mood perk up.

"Yeah." He grabs a salt shaker from one of the cabinets to season the eggs.

"So, you guys were serious last night...about wanting an actual relationship?" I rest my weight on the counter, a bit embarrassed about the question.

"Dead serious," Devlin's voice chimes in behind me.

I turn to look at him and can't help but smirk at his disheveled hair. He looks so sleepy and adorable and sexy. I almost want to jump him again.

He steps up behind me, wrapping his arms around me in a loving embrace. I lean into his touch, completely content.

"We really like you, Rose," he whispers sweetly into my ear. "We want to be with you."

My fear of being used is eradicated as we all eat breakfast together. The conversation flows seamlessly, and I'm amazed at how compatible the three of us are. It wasn't just the alcohol that made us get along so well. There's a genuine connection there. And to be honest, even though we just met, I feel a great affection for them both. They're great, caring and kind, and absolutely incredible in bed.

"Dinner again tonight?" Devlin asks as he escorts me to the door after breakfast.

"You want to see me again so soon?" I can't hide the surprise from my voice.

"See you and do other things to you." He closes in on me, placing his hands on my waist and bending down for a chaste kiss on the lips.

Gareth is by his side, waiting for his turn.

It so weird kissing one man and then another right after. This still doesn't feel real. At any moment, I expect to wake up from the most amazing wet dream.

It's not a wet dream though. They're mine. Both of them. My hot neighbors. And I can't wait to see where this relationship is going to go.

ABOUT THE AUTHOR

Sky Corgan is a USA Today best selling author. When she's not typing away at her next romance novel, she's busy planning for future vacations.

Other Books by Sky Corgan:
Bully
His Possession
Unmatchable
Playing Dom
Damaged
Back to the Heart
The Snowman
Two Much for You
The Billionaires Club
Working for The Billionaires Club
Flesh
Urges
Torn
Strife
Between Two Billionaires
Fifty Shades of BDSM
Jack Kemble
His Indecent Lessons
His Indecent Training
Wrong or Write